MW00951160

Baba and Billy

AND THE
Chocolate Banana Bread

LUC HELTERBRAND

Copyright © 2021 Luc Helterbrand.

All rights reserved. No part of this book may be used or reproduced by any means, graphic, electronic, or mechanical, including photocopying, recording, taping or by any information storage retrieval system without the written permission of the author except in the case of brief quotations embodied in critical articles and reviews.

This is a work of fiction. All of the characters, names, incidents, organizations, and dialogue in this novel are either the products of the author's imagination or are used fictitiously.

Archway Publishing books may be ordered through booksellers or by contacting:

Archway Publishing
1663 Liberty Drive
Bloomington, IN 47403
www.archwaypublishing.com
844-669-3957

Because of the dynamic nature of the Internet, any web addresses or links contained in this book may have changed since publication and may no longer be valid. The views expressed in this work are solely those of the author and do not necessarily reflect the views of the publisher, and the publisher hereby disclaims any responsibility for them.

Any people depicted in stock imagery provided by Getty Images are models, and such images are being used for illustrative purposes only.
Certain stock imagery © Getty Images.

ISBN: 978-1-6657-0675-9 (sc)
ISBN: 978-1-6657-0676-6 (hc)
ISBN: 978-1-6657-0674-2 (e)

Print information available on the last page.

Archway Publishing rev. date: 8/31/2021

ARCHWAY
PUBLISHING

This book is dedicated to the special moments created by children and those who take care of them.

"Baba, I thought bananas are supposed to be yellow!?" Billy exclaimed.

"When they get over ripe, they turn brown and get extra sweet." Baba explained.

"I thought we would make something special with them to share with your mom and dad." Then he began to collect some ingredients from the pantry and turned the oven on to 350 degrees.

As Baba brought over all the ingredients to the table, Billy asked "What are you going to make?"

"Well, you are going to help me, and we are going to make chocolate banana bread!" Baba explained.

"My favorite!" Billy exclaimed, and then asked, "Are we going to use all these things?"

"You bet!" Baba replied, as he continued to place the items on the table.

Baba began by listing out all the things they needed to make the bread...

"We will need one stick of butter, and two eggs, some flour, sugar, salt, vanilla extract, four bananas, dark chocolate chips, and baking soda."

"Then we need a loaf pan, some parchment paper, as well as four bowls, two large ones and two small ones. We will also need a wire mesh strainer, and a hand-mixer, and measuring cups and measuring spoons, a small whisk for eggs, and a spatula for stirring."

First Baba plugged in the mixer and used it to combine the softened butter with the sugar in the first large bowl.

Then Baba took a small bowl and cracked open the eggs into it. He then used the whisk to scramble them and poured that into the creamed butter and sugar.

Next Baba gave Billy a job. He had him peel the four bananas and put them in second large bowl, and then gave him a fork to use to mash them together. It was fun but hard work!

As Billy mashed the bananas, Baba carefully poured the vanilla extract into the teaspoon measuring spoon and added it into the batter.

Once the bananas were mashed, Baba added them to the creamed butter and sugar and Billy stirred them together. That was all the "wet" ingredients.

Next came the "dry" ingredients. Baba placed the wire mesh strainer over the bowl with the wet ingredients and measured out the flour and put that into the strainer. To that he added one teaspoon of baking soda and one-half teaspoon of salt.

Baba told Billy he could pick up the strainer and while holding it over the bowl to gently tap it on the side with his hand.

"Look, Baba! I'm making it snow!" Billy exclaimed and laughed.

Then Baba gave Billy one half measuring cup of dark chocolate chips to add to the bowl and stir into the batter.

As Billy stirred, Baba took another one-half measuring cup of dark chocolate chips, put them into a small bowl. He then put the bowl in the microwave, and melted the chips at 30 second increments, checking each time to make sure they were melting and not burning.

Once the chips were almost completely melted, Baba took a spoon and stirred them until they were smooth and poured them into the batter. Billy stirred the batter till it was smooth.

Then Baba coated the sides and bottom of the inside of the loaf pan with a thin layer of butter.

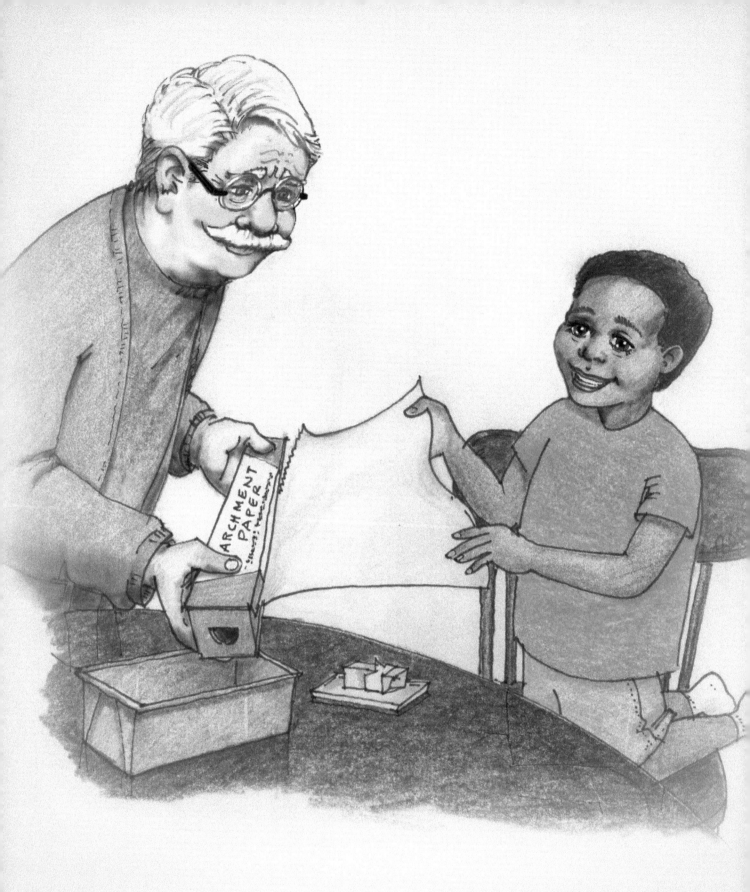

Next Baba took the parchment paper roll and Billy helped him
tear off a piece that was close to the same length as the loaf pan
and placed that into the buttered pan...

... then Baba spread more butter onto the paper that was inside the pan.

"Why did we do this Baba?" Billy asked.

"Doing this will help us get the bread out of the pan easily, without it sticking to the sides!" Baba explained.

Once the pan was lined and greased, Baba poured the batter into the pan carefully. Billy helped by taking the spatula and making sure the last bits of the batter was out of the bowl and in the pan.

Baba then took the loaf pan and placed it on a sheet pan and put them both into the hot oven. He then set the timer to fifty-five minutes.

While the batter baked in the oven, Baba read a book to Billy and after a while, they both fell asleep and took naps.

In a short while, the house filled with the smell of the baking bread and soon the timer chimed so Baba and Billy went into the kitchen to check to see if it was done.

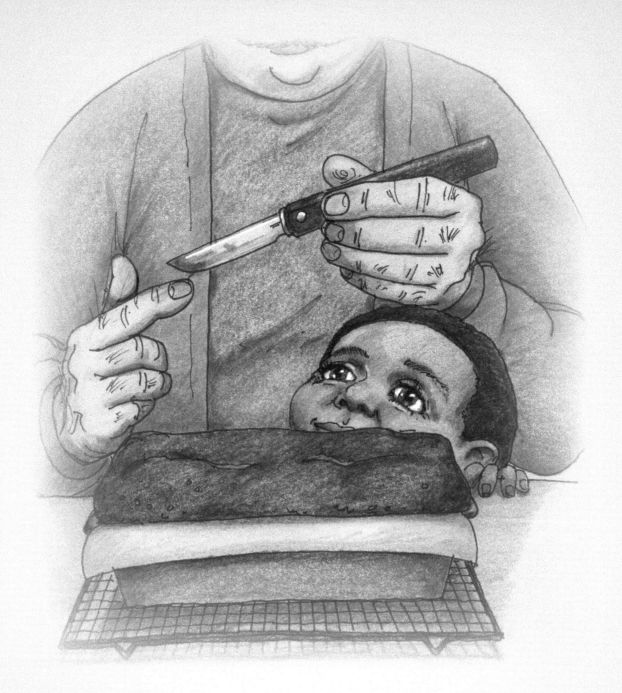

To see if the bread was finished baking, Baba stuck a knife into the center of the loaf.

"Why did you do that, Baba?" Billy asked.

"If the knife comes out mostly clean, then the bread is done, you want to have a little bit of batter on the knife, so you know it's moist...but if there is too much on the knife you need to let it cook a little longer. If there is not anything on the knife, then the bread is overcooked." Baba explained.

Baba decided that the bread was done so he took the loaf pan over to the table and slid the knife between the ends of the bread and the pan and then lifted the bread out of the loaf pan using the parchment paper sides and placed it on a cooling rack. While the bread cooled, Baba and Billy went back to the living room to play.

Not long after, Billy's dad came to take Billy home. Baba cut the loaf in two and gave Billy the bigger half to take home with him. "Thanks Pop!" Billy's dad said as they left.

Later that evening, Billy told his mom and dad about how he helped Baba make the bread. They all enjoyed a slice of chocolate banana bread with some ice cream for dessert...

...and so did Baba.

Baba's Chocolate Banana Bread

Granulated sugar, 1 cup (200 g)

Butter, 1 stick/1/2 cup, softened (227 g)

2 large eggs, beaten (room temperature is best)

4 medium bananas peeled, over ripe and mashed.

Flour – all purpose, sifted, 1 ½ cup (187 g)

Baking soda, 1 teaspoon (5 ml)

Salt, ½ teaspoon (3 ml)

Vanilla extract, 1 teaspoon (5 ml)

Dark or semi-sweet chocolate morsels, ½ cup (227 g) added directly to batter, ½ cup (227 g) melted and added to batter.

Preheat oven to 350F (177C)

Use 9"x5" loaf pan.

See story for instructions.

CPSIA information can be obtained
at www.ICGtesting.com
Printed in the USA
BVHW020951061221
623327BV00022B/964

9 781665 706759